HENRY HOUND

There is no portrait of Henry Hound hanging on the wall of The Towers — so he decides to paint one himself...

British Library Cataloguing in Publication Data

Grant, John, *1930-*
 Henry the artist.
 I. Title   II. Antill, Liz   III. Series
 823'.914[J]
 ISBN 0-7214-1332-3

First edition

Published by Ladybird Books Ltd Loughborough Leicestershire UK
Ladybird Books Inc Auburn Maine 04210 USA

© Illustrations and text LADYBIRD BOOKS LTD MCMXC
Henry Hound © Alton Towers 1988
Printed in England

Henry the Artist

by John Grant
illustrated by Liz Antill

Ladybird Books

Henry was very fond of The Towers, but his favourite part was the picture gallery. He loved to stroll along the gallery and admire the portraits of his ancestors.

There was the ferocious Attila the Hound, Robin Hound with his bow

and arrows, and Admiral Horatio
Hound. Henry's special favourite was
Beau Hound, who was most
handsome, and very elegant.

"There should be a picture of me up
there with the others... Henry
Hound Esq..." thought Henry.

The more Henry thought about it, the better it seemed.

"What's more," he said to himself, "I think I ought to paint it myself. After all, I painted the back door, several windows, and two chairs. All I need is some paint and a few brushes."

He went out to the garden shed. "This could do with a coat of paint," he thought as he opened the door.

On the floor and stacked along the walls were tins of paint in every colour he could want. Henry loaded some into the wheelbarrow, along with several brushes, and went back to the house.

"What I need now," said Henry, "is something to paint on."

In the attic of The Towers there were suits of armour, a stuffed crocodile, and a great many old pictures. There was one picture of a lady with a very badtempered expression.

Henry didn't know who she was, but her picture had a nice frame. It would be a great improvement having his picture in it instead of the badtempered lady.

The picture was too big to carry, so

Henry lowered it from the attic on a rope. Then he propped it up on two chairs and laid out his paint and brushes. Now, he was ready to start.

Henry dipped a brush in the paint... and painted a nose. Next he painted two eyes, a mouth, and the rest of the face in between. After that, he added a pair of very handsome ears.

Then he stood back for a better look. Something wasn't quite right. Either one ear was too big... or the other was too small.

"The trouble
is," he thought,
"I don't know what
I really look like. A mirror
would help."

He fetched a tall mirror. That was
much better, but it still wasn't right.

He thought of the pictures of his ancestors, and suddenly he knew what was wrong. It was the clothes.

Attila the Hound wore a fine sheepskin coat and a spiked helmet. Horatio Hound wore a three-cornered admiral's hat. Beau Hound was most elegant of all, in velvet and lace.

Henry rummaged in the old clothes

chest. He found a long red cloak and
a broad-brimmed hat with a feather
and put them on. Then he picked up
his brush and started painting again.

It went very well, to begin with. But the cloak was heavy and hot and far too big. It kept slipping down over his paw and the brush.

He tried painting with one paw for
the brush and the other holding the
cloak out of the way. That worked
quite well for a while.

Then the dust on the old picture
made him sneeze, and the cloak fell
over his paws.

Henry stopped for a rest and a cup of tea. When he set to work again, he painted the rest of his body, and his legs and feet. Then he painted the long, red cloak.

Now it was time to paint the broad-brimmed hat and the feather.

Henry dipped his brush in the paint and reached up on tiptoe.

He finished the hat, but as he painted the feather something cold and wet ran all over his paw. It was paint, running back down the handle of the brush!

Henry sighed. He wiped his paw
then fetched a stepladder, and stood
it beside the picture. It was heavy,
and felt very shaky.

Henry was beginning to get very hot
and bothered in his hat and cloak.

Taking a deep breath, he climbed to the top step. The stepladder shook alarmingly, but he was almost finished.

With just one more stroke of the brush, the badtempered lady was no more.

Henry looked with admiration at his portrait. He was every bit as handsome as Beau Hound!

Then he saw one small piece he had missed, right up in one corner. If he stretched, he could reach it... just.

He leaned sideways. He leaned a bit further – and the stepladder came down with a crash, Henry with it.

"Help!" he shouted, grabbing at the picture as he fell.

Where Henry had been, there was now a heap of stepladder, picture, chairs, paints and brushes. The heap moved and a green hat appeared, splashed with paint. Under the hat appeared Henry.

"Oh, dear," he thought. "What a shame, and I was just finishing, too."

He started to untangle himself, then he stopped. He could see his picture in its gold frame. It was marvellous! It was so lifelike!

He blinked his eyes. And so did the picture!

Henry wrinkled his nose. So did his portrait! Then he said, "Wait a minute, that's not my portrait at all. It's my reflection in the mirror!"

The picture had fallen on top of him and his head was stuck through a hole in the middle.

He pulled his head out and tidied away the cloak, the hat, and the stepladder. He hid the picture in a dark cupboard. Finally, he wiped up the spilt paint.

Henry loaded the wheelbarrow with
the tins of paint and the brushes and
trundled it back to the garden shed.
"I'm not really a very good artist,
after all. But I *am* very good at the
other kind of painting," he thought
to himself.

So after he had put the paint away, he looked for a big tin of red paint and his biggest brush. Then he set to work to paint the garden shed. And everyone thought it looked lovely!

HENRY HOUND